NATASHA WING'S
The Night Before
My Dance Recital

Grosset & Dunlap
An Imprint of Penguin Random House

To dancers Reina and Karli Krueger and their dance teacher,
Amy Hughes, for their input—NW

To Liv and A.J. . . . who danced even before they could walk—AW

GROSSET & DUNLAP
An Imprint of Penguin Random House LLC, New York

Penguin supports copyright. Copyright fuels creativity, encourages diverse voices, promotes free speech, and creates a vibrant culture.
Thank you for buying an authorized edition of this book and for complying with copyright laws by not reproducing, scanning, or distributing any
part of it in any form without permission. You are supporting writers and allowing Penguin to continue to publish books for every reader.

Text copyright © 2015 by Natasha Wing. Illustrations copyright © 2015 by Penguin Random House LLC. All rights reserved.
Published by Grosset & Dunlap, an imprint of Penguin Random House LLC, New York.
GROSSET & DUNLAP is a trademark of Penguin Random House LLC. Manufactured in China.

Visit us online at www.penguinrandomhouse.com.
Library of Congress Control Number: 2015956297

ISBN 9780448488455   10 9 8 7 6 5 4 3 2

NATASHA WING'S
The Night Before
My Dance Recital

By Natasha Wing
Illustrated by Amy Wummer

Grosset & Dunlap
An Imprint of Penguin Random House

'Twas the night before the recital,
and all across the stage,

my dance class was lined up
by height, not by age.

We've practiced for months; we know how each step goes.

Just look how we pirouette and point our fingers and toes!

"Let's skip! Now turn! All step to the beat!
Now soar! Now fly! Dancers, pick up those feet!
To the front of the stage, circle back to the wall!
Now dance away! Dance away! Dance away all!"

"I missed a step," I told my teacher once rehearsal was done.
"You'll get it," she said, and we practiced one-on-one.

That night I tossed about in my bed,
while visions of arabesques danced in my head.

I woke with a start.

What if I ruin the show?

If I mess up my steps,
everyone will know!

It was buzzing like crazy in the girls' dressing room.
I quickly changed from my clothes into my gorgeous costume.

When what to my twinkling eyes should appear—
a complete transformation, that much was clear.

My wings—how they fluttered! My feathers—shimmery green!
I was the most glorious bird the world's ever seen!

Mom bobby-pinned my bun
and set it with hair spray.

She fastened my tiara
and hoped it would stay.

Then she brushed on some makeup,
adding lipstick and blush.
My dance teacher clapped.
"Hurry, hurry! Please rush!"

We each took our places. We were ready to go.
It was now time for us to put on a show!

The theater lights dimmed.
The music had started.

We all smiled big smiles.
And then—the curtains parted!

I performed the dance steps

and leaped with all of my might.

But when everyone twirled left . . .
Oops! I spun right!

Did the audience giggle?
I didn't hear a thing.
I was a beautiful bird
and kept flapping each wing.

I quickly got back in step; I magically hit my stride.

At the end of the show, we were bursting with pride!

The girls did deep curtsies,
while the boys took a bow.
We got a standing ovation.
We were all stars now!

Our parents gave us flowers,
and friends cheered, "Bravo!"
My brother even told me
it was a really cool show.

For me, the recital
was the funnest—times ten!
I can't wait to perform
onstage once again!